CU00847066

BUCKLEY GOES TO THE BEACH

Buckley Goes to the Beach

WRITTEN AND ILLUSTRATED BY TONY SQUIRE

S.A.Squire & T.Squire

Copyright © 2022 by

All rights reserved. No part of this book may be reproduced in any manner whatsoever without written permission except in the case of brief quotations embodied in critical articles and reviews.

First Printing, 2022

Some of the characters and events portrayed in this book are based on real people, whilst others, including spoken word, are fictitious. Any similarity to real persons, living or dead, is coincidental and not intended by the author.

In September of 2021 I was invited to speak at Our Lady of Dolours Primary School in Mitchelton, which is a suburb of Brisbane. I had a wonderful experience chatting to the pupils and telling them all about my books and how I came to create my character, Buckley the Yowie. As part of my visit I created a competition in which students were asked to think of a title for a Buckley the Yowie story. The prize was a signed copy of my book, 'Buckley the Yowie and the Legend of Ned Kelly', a signed copy of the story written as a result of their idea, as well as the winner being a character in my book.

Needless to say, the industrious and enthusiastic children of Our Lady of Dolours School did not let me down, and I was flooded with some brilliant ideas, for which I am grateful. As the competition was a two part one, being for one student from grades Prep to 3, and one from grades 4 to 6, there were two winners. This particular title was the idea of a young man by the name of Michael Dutton, who appears as Michael in the story.

I would, therefore, like to thank Michael very much for his very clever idea, and also to dedicate this story to him. Congratulations Michael, I hope you enjoy reading about Buckley's day at the beach...........with you!

This is Buckley the Yowie. As you can see he is *very* tall. In fact he is more than three metres tall; and that *is* big.

Do you like to go to the beach? Buckley does, but, sadly, he always seems to end up on his own, because people think he is a scary monster, so they run off screaming, making such a fuss. Silly people!

Now, *we* know that Buckley is a very nice fellow and a friend to everyone, so there is no reason to be afraid.

This is Michael. Say hello. He is one of Buckley's friends from the town of Kilcoy. Michael has come to the seaside with his parents so that he can show Buckley all of the fun things to do at the beach. How kind he is.

"The beach is a fun place," said Michael, "what do *you* like to do at the beach Buckley?" Buckley scratched his head and had a bit of a think. "I love to fish," he replied. Michael agreed that fishing is fun but knew that there was *so* much more to do. "Take my hand Buckley and I will show you," said Michael.

Michael is right about the fun to be had, but all of a sudden Buckley said "Stop!" Buckley then picked up a squeezy bottle of sun screen. "The sun is very hot and you can get burned," he told Michael, "so the first thing you must always do at the beach is to put sun screen on your skin. You know......slip, slap and slop". No sooner had he spoken, Buckley was squirting sun screen on to Michael. "There you go, rub it in. That will keep you safe," said Buckley to his friend.

The first fun thing on Michael's list was to grab his bucket and spade, and make a sand castle. "Buckley," look at my sand castle," said a proud Michael. "Wow! That is great. Can I have a go please?" replied an excited Buckley.

Buckley was so excited about making his first sand castle that he began work right away. There was sand flying everywhere, and when it was all finished Buckley stood proudly next to his *very* tall castle. "That is huge," said Michael, "in fact it is so big that you could live in it".

"That was fun," said Buckley, "what else can we do now?" An idea came to Michael as he saw some very large shells. He picked one up, held it to his ear, and smiled. "If you close your eyes and listen, you can hear the sea," said Michael.

Now, Buckley thought that a little odd, and pointed at the water. "Look, there is the sea just there, and I can hear it very well, and do not need a shell," he said, feeling a little confused. Buckley then had an idea, bent down, picked up a shell and began to blow in to it. "See," he said, "I am making music with *my* shell".

Michael had to put his fingers in his ears, as Buckley was not very musical at all, and was making a terrible noise with his shell. But, at least he was trying, and he *was* having fun.

"Come on Buckley, I have much more to show you. Can you skip?" said Michael. "Skip?" replied Buckley, "I've never tried. Let's give it a go". Michael had brought some ropes with him and very soon he and Buckley were skipping on the beach like Kangaroos.

"That was fun," said Buckley, "shall we use your spade to make more sand castles?"
"I have an even better idea," said Michael, "lie down and relax and I will show you".
Always keen for a quick snooze, Buckley lay down on the beach and was soon fast
asleep, dreaming of fishing.

When Buckley awoke he was feeling very itchy and wet for, while he was sleeping,
Michael had buried him up to his head in sand.

Buckley smiled, but did not enjoy being buried at all. There was sand everywhere! In his fur, under in his finger nails and even in his board shorts. Buckley sprang from the sand. "Right. Time to get this sand off me," he said. Buckley and Michael ran in to the sea. As Buckley was washing off the sand, Michael had other ideas, and began to splash water at Buckley. At first Buckley thought that his friend was being helpful, but soon realised there was fun to be had, so they spent the next few minutes splashing each other, until they were well and truly soaked. Oh what fun they had.

As Buckley and Michael were now very wet, they decided that it was time for a swim. Grabbing their floaties, they ran in to the warm sea, where they swam and paddled together for ages.

While they were swimming, Buckley saw that there was much fun to be had in the water, as well as on the beach. So he and Michael had lots of fun, in the shallows, paddling around in a rubber boat.

They had even more fun surfing the waves close to the sea shore. Look at them go!

As Buckley gazed out to the horizon, he was amazed. Very quickly he could see that the beach was not just a place for children and Yowies to enjoy themselves. It was a place for grownups too.

He could see a lady standing on some sticks while being pulled along by a fast boat. Michael told him that this was called water skiing. Buckley also saw some people riding on what looked like motor bikes. He was surprised that they didn't sink. This made Michael laugh, but he explained that they were called jet skis. Whatever they were, Buckley wanted to have a go. "They are not things for me to do just yet as I am too small, but Mum says you should have a go. She wants me to put my T-shirt on anyway," said Michael.

Buckley didn't need to be asked twice and was soon riding a jet ski, bouncing across the waves, as Michael watched from the safety of the beach.

He even managed to do some water skiing and had a great time. Look at Buckley go!
Woo hoo!

Michael could see, by the big grin on Buckley's face, that he had enjoyed bouncing around on the waves, and was eager for more.

Michael handed Buckley a large ring. "What's this?" asked Buckley, scratching his head. "It's called a hula hoop," replied Michael, "you twirl it around your waist and try to keep it from dropping to the ground". "That sounds simple enough," said Buckley, as he began spinning the hula hoop around his waist. He did drop it a few times but eventually got the hang of it and had a great time.

"What's next?" asked Buckley, who was hungry for more fun things to do.

"Gosh Buckley, you really are full of beans. How about some beach games?" said Michael.

Buckley was up for anything, so he and Michael spent the rest of the day playing ball games.

Buckley enjoyed beach baseball and was hitting home runs with every ball.

Do *you* like to play bat and ball games? They are fun aren't they?

Next Buckley had a go at beach tennis and was jumping and flying around like a super hero, hitting the ball here, there, and everywhere. Look at him go!

They played catch with Michael's beach ball.

Then ran along the beach, whilst flying a kite in the sea breeze. Wow, look at it fly! What a busy day they had.

But all good things must come to an end, and Buckley thanked his friend for a great day. "There certainly is a lot of fun to be had at the beach, but with all of this swimming, hula hooping, running, jumping and skipping I am feeling a little tired," said Buckley.

As the daylight was fading, the two friends sat quietly on the beach watching the sunset, whilst listening to sounds of the waves lapping the shore, and the noisy seagulls screeching.

Both agreed that at the end of the day when you are tired after all of the fun, it's always great to sit quietly with a friend or loved one, and watch the going down of the sun.

See you next time.

About The Author

Tony Squire is the creator of Buckley, the world's favourite Yowie, who appeared in his first story, Buckley the Kilcoy Yowie, in 2019. Although originally intended to be a character for primary/high school children, the tales of Buckley the Yowie soon became popular with younger children when the author began to write short stories and picture book readers. Buckley is fast becoming one of the best loved pre and primary school characters of all time, and his stories and adventures are enjoyed the world over.

Tony was born on 6 November 1962, in Reading, England. Being the son of a professional soldier, Tony lived in five different countries, and was educated at sixteen schools worldwide. At school he particularly enjoyed history and art, which later resulted in his creation of Buckley, both in word and shape, and the insertion of his character in to real historical events. Tony's intention was always to create a fun story in which children have a both enjoyable and learning experience, whether it be about history, diversity or just plain good old fashioned morals and attitudes.

The design of Buckley the Yowie was inspired by the statue of the Kilcoy Yowie in the town of Kilcoy, Queensland, Australia, which depicts the Yowie as a man, not a monster. Tony hopes that through Buckley's innocence, fun spirit, and magic, children will enjoy reading and learning at the same time.

The magical Buckley is becoming hugely popular and a series of adventures has followed, including the introduction of Buckley's friends and adopted family. Buckley has expanded from the original short stories, to a novel about Buckley's friendship with the notorious outlaw Ned Kelly, and several reading books.

Tony is the sole driving force in the development of all Buckley the Yowie projects at every stage.

He and his wife Sheila reside in Woolmar, Queensland, which is just outside of Kilcoy; Yowie country. Conversations and memories from their childhoods provide continual inspiration for the Buckley stories.

Tony hopes that children of all ages will grow to love his stories and pass on the love to their own children.

More Books By This Author

For the pre-schooler:

'I'm Buckley and I'm a Yowie'.
'Buckley the Yowie Loves Christmas'.

For early years school children:

'Crossing the Road with Buckley the Yowie'.
'Stop Snoring Buckley!'
Ít's Halloween Buckley!'
'Buckley Goes to the Beach'.

When you get bigger you might like to read:

'Buckley the Kilcoy Yowie'.
'Buckley's Return'.
'Buckley Saves Christmas'.

When you get even bigger still, you might like to read:

'Buckley the Yowie and the Legend of Ned Kelly'.

CPSIA information can be obtained
at www.ICGtesting.com
Printed in the USA
LVHW071049040422
715245LV00002B/48